minedition

English edition published 2018 by
Michael Neugebauer Publishing Ltd., Hong Kong

Michael Neugebauer Publishing Ltd.,
Unit 28, 5/F, Metro Centre, Phase 2, No.21 Lam Hing Street, Kowloon Bay, Kowloon, Hong Kong.
Phone +852 2807 1711, e-mail: info@minedition.com
This edition was printed in July 2017 at L.Rex Printing Co Ltd.
3/F., Blue Box Factory Bldg, 25 Hing Wo Street, Tin Wan, Aberdeen, Hong Kong, China
Typesetting in Sabon
Library of Congress Cataloging-in-Publication Data available upon request.

ISBN 978-988-8341-09-2
10 9 8 7 6 5 4 3 2 1 First Impression

For more information please visit our website: www.minedition.com

Marcus Herrenberger

Little Rabbit Has Friends

translated by Kathryn Bishop

minedition

"Wren, you may have a crown because you're so clever," said the raven, "but I'll bet you don't know what I know."

"Perhaps you should tell me then," said the little bird.

"Well, the fox made an announcement. He is planning to eat Little Rabbit. Today! What do you think about that? Little Rabbit is your friend, isn't he?"

"Oh, no," said Wren. "I mean, yes, the rabbit is my friend! I can't let this happen."

"You?" squawked the raven. "Don't you think the fox will eat you, too? He is strong and more than just clever."

Wren flew to find Mouse.

"Have you heard, Mouse?" asked Wren.
"The fox told the raven he's going to eat Little Rabbit today!"

"What?" peeped the mouse. "Little Rabbit is our friend. Oh, this is awful.
We should do something. But if the fox eats Little Rabbit he might eat...
he might eat... oh, Wren, I'm afraid!"

Mouse was trembling as the bird tried to calm him. "It would be terrible,
but we are all friends! No, I won't let the fox eat you, or Little Rabbit either."

Mouse and Wren met the hedgehog and the nuthatch and told them that the fox was planning to eat their friend, Little Rabbit.

Hedgehog thought about it and said, "That's so mean. Little Rabbit has no chance at all. That fox is as fast as lightning and has terrible teeth. I feel so sorry for our Little Rabbit."

"Squirrel, have you heard?" asked the wren. "The rabbit, our Little Rabbit, the fox plans to eat him, today. What would our forest be like without Little Rabbit?"

"Oh, how dreadful, that nasty old fox," said the squirrel. "A forest without Little Rabbit would be so sad and empty. But what can we do? First, he'll eat the Little Rabbit, then me, then Mouse and then–then he will eat you!"

"Do you think he'd eat me too?" asked the wren.

"Little Rabbit, did you hear
the news?" asked the mouse.
"This morning the fox told the raven... Well...
he told him he would eat you. Today!"

Little Rabbit began to cry.

"I have no chance against that fox," he sobbed. "He will eat me for sure.
Oh, this is terrible! This world was so beautiful."

Wren flew to the wild pig family to ask for help. "Have you heard, the fox wants to eat our friend Little Rabbit? Please help us, please. You are so strong."

"Does he know about it already, has someone told him?" asked the mama pig.

One of the little piglets said, "Mama, this can't happen. Little Rabbit is our friend, and he is so very little."

"Yes, my dear, he is our friend," said Mama Pig, "but that fox is so fast and smart and strong. I do not want him to eat you both! No, I'm afraid the fox will get to eat Little Rabbit today."

The wild pig wouldn't help.

What could they do? There were five of them, but they were far too weak to defeat a fox.

So Wren, Nuthatch, Hedgehog, Mouse and Squirrel went to visit Little Rabbit and say their goodbyes.

The frightened little rabbit waited sadly. He couldn't move, for if the fox saw him, he would surely catch him.

Then the fox, with his terribly sharp teeth, was suddenly standing right in front of him. The frightened little rabbit knew he was done for.

And then it happened.

"If you want to eat Little Rabbit," shouted Mouse, "you're going to have to deal with us."

The fox's expression changed. He actually looked frightened. Wren flew at the fox and pooped on his nose.

"Take that," said Wren.

Mouse squeaked wildly at the fox, and Mama Pig stood in front of him, strong and furious.

The fox turned, ran, and was never seen in the woods again.
They had all chased him away.

"Well," the mole asked, "what happened?"

"Everything's okay," said Little Rabbit. "We did it; together we did it. The fox is gone."

"Children," Mama Pig said, "it's getting late. Time for bed."

"See you tomorrow," said Little Rabbit, "and thank you, everyone! It's wonderful to have such brave friends."